Tiptoe Into Scary Cities

NIGHTMARISH NEW YORK

by E. Merwin

Consultant: Debbie Felton
Professor of Classics
University of Massachusetts
Amherst, Massachusetts

BEARPORT PUBLISHING

New York, New York

Credits

Cover, © Boudikka/Shutterstock, © Francois Roux/Shutterstock, Sorapop Udomsri/Shutterstock, © Niels Vos/Shutterstock, and © John Blous/Shutterstock; TOC, © f11photo/Shutterstock; 4–5, © baranozdemir/iStock, © Dja65/Shutterstock, © photo one/Shutterstock, © borsmenta/Shutterstock, and © Roman Bodnarchuk/Shutterstock; 6, Public Domain; 7, © Jean Leon Gerome Ferris/Library of Congress/Public Domain; 8T, © Attributed to Hendrick Couturier/Public Domain; 8B, © kazu326/Shutterstock; 9, © Momos/CC BY-SA 4.0; 10–11, © Everett Historical/Shutterstock; 11B, © T photography/Shutterstock; 12, © Rusty Elliott/Dreamstime; 13, © Library and Archives Canada; 14, Matthew Brady/Public Domain; 15, © Beyond My Ken/GFDL; 16–17, © Garn Donati/Shutterstock; 17L, © EricVega/iStock; 18, © Donna Beeler/Shutterstock; 19T, © Stocksnapper/Shutterstock; 19B, © Steve Sands/AP Images; 20L, © Maurice Savage/Alamy; 20R, © Laura Saleri/Shutterstock; 21, © Mario Mitsis/Alamy; 23, © Ruben Martinez Barricarte/Shutterstock; 24, © LiskaM/Shutterstock and © Alexey Bukreev/Shutterstock.

Publisher: Kenn Goin
Senior Editor: Joyce Tavolacci
Creative Director: Spencer Brinker
Photo Researcher: Thomas Persano
Cover: Kim Jones

Library of Congress Cataloging-in-Publication Data in process at time of publication (2019)
Library of Congress Control Number: 2018009276
ISBN-13: 978-1-68402-664-7 (library binding)

For more information, write to Bearport Publishing Company, Inc., 45 West 21st Street, Suite 3B, New York, New York 10010.

Contents

NIGHTMARISH NEW YORK

New York City is often called "the City That Never Sleeps." While many New Yorkers are up all night, so, too, are the city's ghosts. For hundreds of years, millions of people have lived—and died—in the city. If you take a tour, watch out for **phantoms**!

Get ready to read four spooky stories about New York City. Turn the page . . . if you dare.

"Old Silver Leg"

St. Mark's Church in-the-Bowery

Long ago, New York was called New Amsterdam. In 1647, a tough man named Peter Stuyvesant was **governor.** After a cannonball blew off his leg, Peter wore a wooden peg. The peg was made with silver bands, so he was known as "Old Silver Leg."

New Amsterdam

In 1672, Peter died. He was buried in a **crypt.** But Old Silver Leg didn't stay there for long!

Peter "Old Silver Leg" Stuyvesant

Soon after his death, workers saw Peter's **spirit** roaming throughout his house. One night, there was a fire. The next morning, a peg-legged ghost was seen staring into the ashes.

Peter Stuyvesant

Many years later, St. Mark's Church was built near Peter's grave. Often, the sound of his peg leg is heard *tap, tap, tapping* along the church's old stone floor.

St. Mark's Church in-the-Bowery

In 1995, a strange voice echoed in the church. Then a man appeared who seemed to have walked through a wall! Many believe it was Peter's spirit.

Haunted Halls

Ellis Island

New York City has always welcomed **immigrants.** In the early 1900s, they came by ship. Their first stop was Ellis Island. After a long journey, some people arrived ill. They were sent to a hospital on the island. Many never left. . . .

Immigrants on Ellis Island in the early 1900s

Ellis Island today

Hundreds of immigrants died soon after landing in New York. Many were small children. In recent times, workers have heard kids' voices in empty buildings on the island. Doors have been seen slamming on their own. Do the spirits of the children still haunt the island?

Near Ellis Island is the Statue of Liberty. Strange lights have been seen above it. There are also reports of ghostly faces in the crown of the statue.

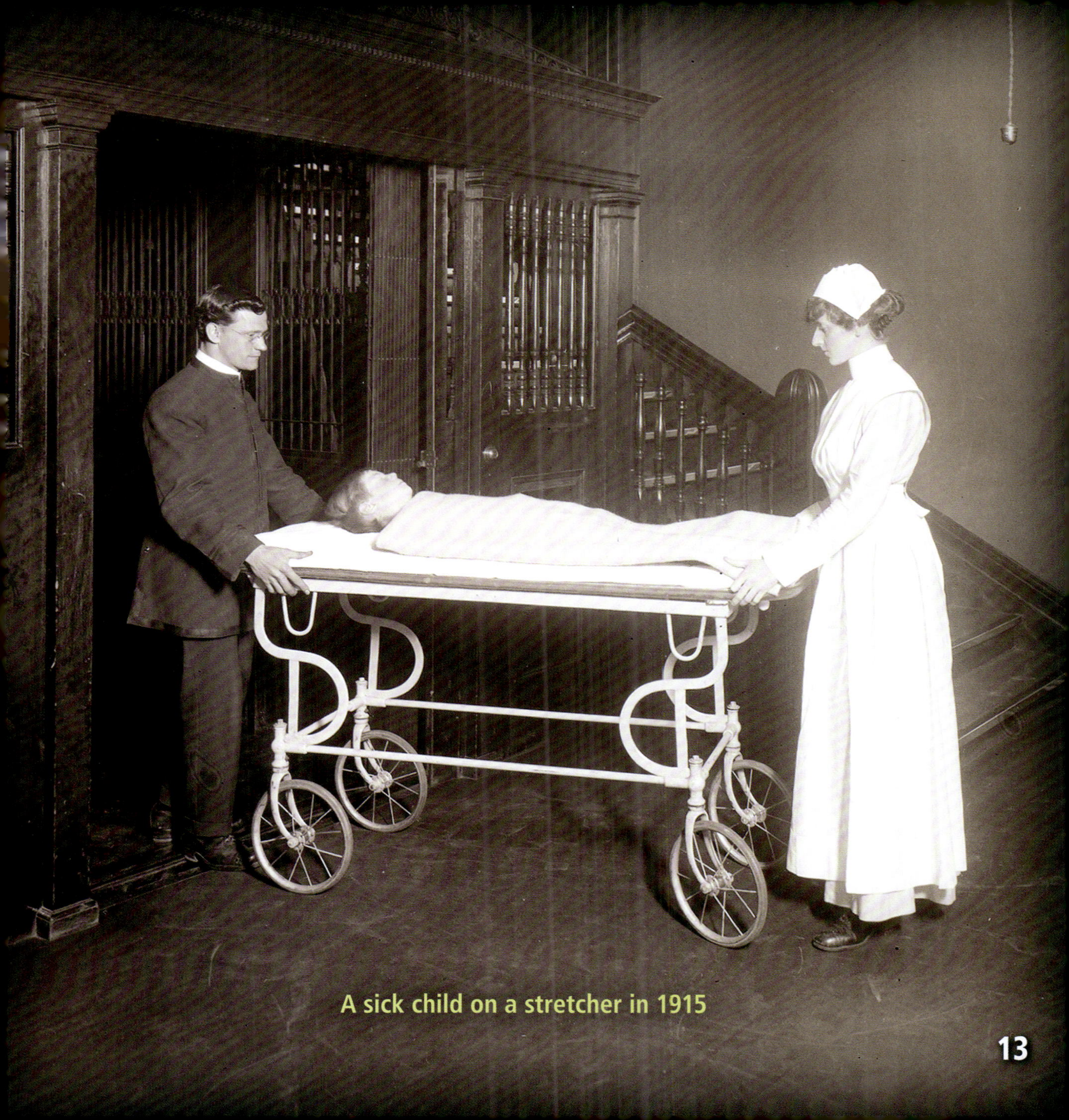

A sick child on a stretcher in 1915

Two Ghastly Ghosts

New York University

New York University (NYU) has many students on its **campus** . . . and maybe a few ghosts. The most famous is author Edgar Allan Poe.

In 1845, Poe lived in a building that's now part of NYU. Today, this long-dead writer is known to surprise students on the staircase. He's also said to haunt the dreams of anyone who sets foot in the building.

Edgar Allan Poe wrote scary stories.

NYU's Furman Hall, also known as Poe House

Brittany Hall is a haunted NYU **dormitory.** One hundred years ago, it was a hotel. Back then, a young girl was playing when she fell down an elevator **shaft** and died. Her name was Molly, and her spirit is still said to wander the building.

At night, Molly is heard tapping on walls and humming. Is the lonely ghost looking for someone to play with her?

In 2016, an NYU student was in her room with friends. Suddenly, the door flew open. “We don’t want to play now Molly,” the student shouted back. The door slammed shut!

Stars and Spirits

The Dakota

The Dakota is an apartment building in Manhattan. It's been home to many stars—and spirits!

From 1973 to 1980, music star John Lennon and his wife, Yoko Ono, lived in the Dakota. John often saw ghosts in the building. He called one sad spirit the Crying Lady. He also used to see a ghostly girl bouncing a ball.

The Dakota

Yoko Ono and John Lennon

Sadly, in 1980, John was shot and killed outside the Dakota. Three years later, a neighbor bumped into John's ghost! It was bathed in a bright, white light.

The place where John Lennon was shot

Before he died, John saw a **UFO** outside his window. At least seven other people described the same red object in the sky.

Thirteen years later, John's spirit visited Yoko. She saw him sitting at his piano. Turning to her, he said, "Don't be afraid. I am still with you." Then, he **vanished**!

John Lennon at his piano

Spooky Spots in New York City

New York University
Students get to graduate from NYU, but some ghosts never leave.

Ellis Island
This island is a favorite haunt for visitors—and a few phantoms.

The Dakota
This famous building has been home to many stars—alive and dead!

St. Mark's Church in-the-Bowery
Do you dare take a seat in this spooky spot?

Glossary

campus (KAM-puhss) the land and buildings that make up a school

crypt (KRIPT) an underground room where people are often buried

dormitory (DOR-muh-tor-ee) a building where students live and sleep on a college campus

governor (GUHV-er-ner) the head of a state

immigrants (IM-uh-gruhntz) people who come from one country to live in another

phantoms (FAN-tuhmz) ghosts or spirits

shaft (SHAFT) a tall empty space or passageway that houses an elevator

spirit (SPIHR-it) a supernatural being, such as a ghost

UFO (YOO EFF OH) Unidentified Flying Object, something seen in the air that cannot be explained

vanished (VAN-ishd) disappeared from sight

Index

Read More

Markovics, Joyce. *Chilling Cemeteries (Tiptoe Into Scary Places).* New York: Bearport (2017).

Zullo, Allan. *Haunted Kids: True Ghost Stories.* New York: Scholastic (2000).

Learn More Online

To learn more about Nightmarish New York, visit:
www.bearportpublishing.com/Tiptoe

About the Author

E. Merwin enjoys researching haunted histories. As for the ghosts, she wishes them well in this world—and the next.